As
Babies
Dream

For my mother and father, in loving memory—LN
To Eva, dream big little one!—TM

Books for Kids From the
American Psychological Association
maginationpress.org

Text copyright © 2021 by Lesléa Newman. A version of the text first appeared in *Here's A Little Poem* edited by Jane Yolen and Andrew Fusek Peters; Candlewick, 2007. Illustrations copyright © 2021 by Taia Morley. Published in 2021 by Magination Press, an imprint of the American Psychological Association All rights reserved. Except as permitted under the United States Copyright Act of 1976, no part of this publication may be reproduced or distributed in any form or by any means, or stored in a database or retrieval system, without the prior written permission of the publisher.

Magination Press is a registered trademark of the American Psychological Association. Order books at maginationpress.org or call 1-800-374-2721.

Printed by Phoenix Color, Hagerstown, MD

Library of Congress Cataloging-in-Publication Data
Names: Newman, Lesléa, author. | Morley, Taia, illustrator.
Title: As babies dream / by Lesléa Newman ; illustrated by Taia Morley.
Description: Washington, DC : Magination Press, [2021] | Audience: Ages 4-8. | Audience: Grades 2-3. | Summary: In this rhyming lullaby, animal and human parents show unconditional love for their babies.
Identifiers: LCCN 2021004687 (print) | LCCN 2021004688 (ebook) | ISBN 9781433836817 (hardcover) | ISBN 9781433836831 (ebook)
  Subjects: CYAC: Stories in rhyme. | Bedtime—Fiction. | Parent and child—Fiction. | Parental behavior in animals—Fiction. | Babies—Fiction. | Love—Fiction.
  Classification: LCC PZ8.3.N4655 As 2021 (print) | LCC PZ8.3.N4655 (ebook) | DDC [E]—dc23
  LC record available at https://lccn.loc.gov/2021004687
  LC ebook record available at https://lccn.loc.gov/2021004688

  Manufactured in the United States of America
  10 9 8 7 6 5 4 3 2 1

As Babies Dream

By Lesléa Newman
Illustrated by Taia Morley

As the crows fly

and the rivers flow,

As the eagles cry

and the winds blow,

As the hawks soar

and the frogs leap,

As the lions roar

and the lambs sleep,

As the turtles sun

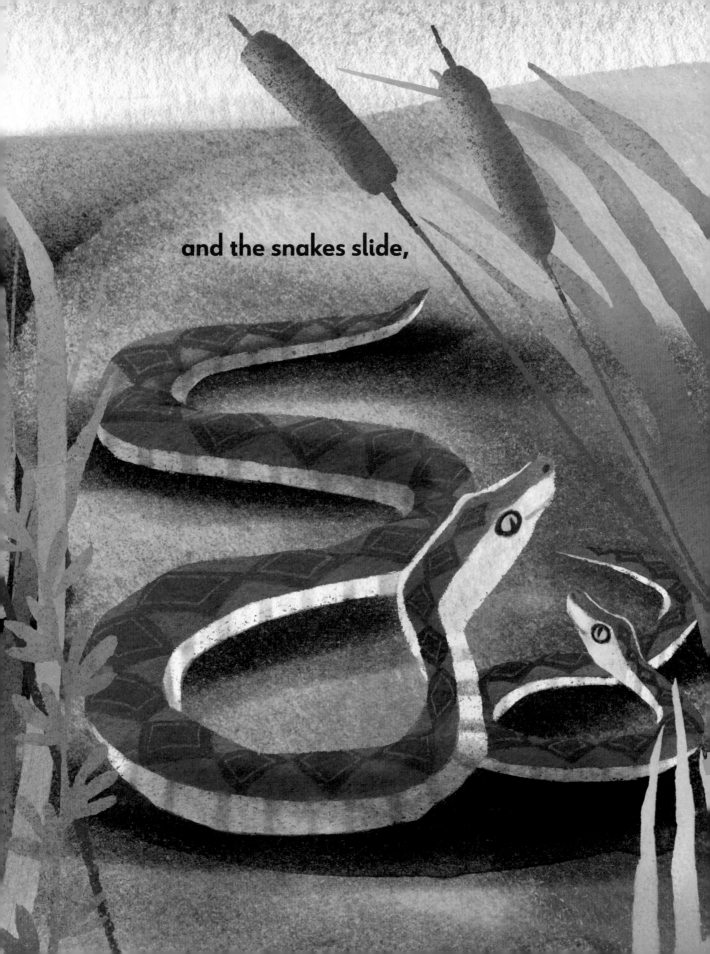

and the snakes slide,

As the horses run

and the swans glide,

As the rabbits hop

and the owls call,

As the leaves drop and the rains fall,

As the rainbows arc

and the willows sway,

As the dogs bark

and the wolves bay,

As the cattle doze

and the night begins,

As the moon glows

and the earth spins,

As the stars gleam

high up above,

the babies dream

safe in our love.

Lesléa Newman has created 75 books for readers of all ages, including the children's books *Sparkle Boy, Remembering Ethan,* and *Heather Has Two Mommies.* She has received two National Jewish Book Awards, two Association of Jewish Libraries Sydney Taylor Awards, and the Massachusetts Book Award. She is also a past poet laureate of Northampton, MA. Visit lesleakids.com and @LesleaNewman on Twitter.

Taia Morley is an illustrator who works on a variety of projects, from children's books to packaging art to toys and bookmobiles. She lives in St. Paul, MN. Visit taiamorley.com, @TaiaMorleyIllustration on Facebook, and @TaiaMorley on Twitter and Instagram.

Magination Press is the children's book imprint of the American Psychological Association. APA works to advance psychology as a science and profession and as a means of promoting health and human welfare. Magination Press books reach young readers and their parents and caregivers to make navigating life's challenges a little easier. It's the combined power of psychology and literature that makes a Magination Press book special. Visit maginationpress.org and @MaginationPress on Facebook, Twitter, Instagram, and Pinterest.